The
Tiara
Club
at Silver
Towers

For my very own Princess Alice,
with all my love, Mom
xx VF

For Janet
and little Prince Leandro
x SG

www.tiaraclub.co.uk

ORCHARD BOOKS
338 Euston Road, London NW1 3BH
Orchard Books Australia
Hachette Children's Books
Level 17/207 Kent St, Sydney NSW 2000

A Paperback Original

First published in Great Britain in 2006
Text © Vivian French 2006
Illustrations © Sarah Gibb 2006

A CIP catalogue record for this book is available
from the British Library.

ISBN 978 1 84616 198 8

5 7 9 10 8 6 4

The Tiara Club at Silver Towers

Princess Alice

and the Crystal Slipper

By Vivian French

Illustrated by Sarah Gibb

CLASS: Φ JF;FRE

NUMBER: J1600241848

ORCHARD BOOKS

2006   £3.99   GIFT

The Royal Palace Academy
for the Preparation of Perfect Princesses

(Known to our students as *"The Princess Academy"*)

OUR SCHOOL MOTTO:
A Perfect Princess always thinks of others
before herself, and is kind, caring and truthful.

Silver Towers offers a complete education for Tiara Club princesses with emphasis on selected outings. The curriculum includes:

Fans and Curtseys	*Problem Prime Ministers*
A visit to Witch Windlespin	*A visit to the Museum of Royal Life*
(Royal herbalist, healer and maker of magic potions)	*(Students will be well protected from the Poisoned Apple)*

Our headteacher, Queen Samantha Joy, is present at all times, and students are well looked after by the school Fairy Godmother, Fairy Angora.

Our resident staff and visiting experts include:

LADY ALBINA MacSPLINTER *(School Secretary)*	*QUEEN MOTHER MATILDA* *(Etiquette, Posture and Poise)*
CROWN PRINCE DANDINO *(School Excursions)*	*FAIRY G* *(Head Fairy Godmother)*

We award tiara points to encourage our Tiara Club princesses towards the next level. All princesses who win enough points at Silver Towers will attend the Silver Ball, where they will be presented with their Silver Sashes.

Silver Sash Tiara Club princesses are invited to return to Ruby Mansions, our exclusive residence for Perfect Princesses, where they may continue their education at a higher level.

PLEASE NOTE:
Princesses are expected to arrive at
the Academy with a *minimum* of:

TWENTY BALL GOWNS
(with all necessary hoops,
petticoats, etc)

TWELVE DAY DRESSES

SEVEN GOWNS
suitable for garden parties,
and other special
day occasions

TWELVE TIARAS

DANCING SHOES
five pairs

VELVET SLIPPERS
three pairs

RIDING BOOTS
two pairs

Cloaks, muffs, stoles, gloves
and other essential
accessories as required

Hi! How are you doing? It's so brilliant that you're here at Silver Towers - you're a real STAR. Not like the twins - Princess Diamonde and Princess Gruella. They're SO stuck-up and horrible. Sometimes I almost hope they won't get enough tiara points to win their Silver Sashes and go on to Ruby Mansions...but that's NOT the way a Perfect Princess ought to think!

Oh - I forgot to say. I'm Princess Alice and I share the Silver Rose Room with Charlotte, Katie, Daisy, Sophia and Emily. They're my best friends, and we try to do everything together...

Chapter One

Do you go on school outings? Ever since we've been at Silver Towers we've had one trip out after another. Our headteacher, Queen Samantha Joy, says that it's good for us – and they usually do end up being quite fun! But we were SERIOUSLY excited when Queen Samantha Joy told us we were going to go to King Rudolfo the Third's private Museum of Royal Life. My big sis went there when she was at Silver Towers (she's at Ruby Mansions now) and she said it was AMAZING! She saw the Poisoned Apple, and the Crystal Slipper, and the Spinning Wheel – and loads of other really fantastic things.

Lady Albina (she's Queen Samantha Joy's secretary, and organises us with about fifty thousand lists every single day) heard me telling my friends about the museum after morning assembly was over, and frowned at me. She's always frowning, unless she's talking to Queen Samantha Joy.

"Princess Alice, I do hope you don't think you know everything already!" she snapped.

I heard Princess Diamonde snigger, and whisper, "SHE doesn't, but WE do, don't we?" to Gruella, but I pretended I hadn't heard.

"Oh no! I really don't," I said, and curtsied to Lady Albina.

"I'm glad to hear it! That is how mistakes are made! Tomorrow you will be divided into groups. Each group will have a questionnaire to complete, and tiara points will be awarded for the best entries. And—" Lady Albina looked even more disapproving – "King Rudolfo has offered a prize. A QUITE unnecessary kindness, if you ask me."

"A PRIZE?" We clustered round
Lady Albina. Even Diamonde and
Gruella looked excited. "Please,
Lady Albina – WHAT prize?"

Lady Albina sniffed. "The winning group will be invited to take part in King Rudolfo's Annual Royal Parade. They will, I understand, ride in the Golden Pumpkin Coach."

A royal parade! And a golden pumpkin coach! It sounded SO wonderful. We couldn't help talking about it every time we had a spare moment in between lessons, and that night we were MUCH too excited to sleep.

"We will be in the same group, won't we?" Daisy asked. It would be SO awful if we weren't."

"Of course we will be," Emily

said comfortingly. "Lady Albina chooses by dormitories."

"Hurrah! for the Silver Rose Roomers!" Katie cheered. "And you know all about the museum, Alice – so we'll have a really good chance of winning."

I shook my head. "I only know what my big sis said."

"Is everything in glass cases?" Charlotte asked. "Or can we touch them?"

"NO!' Sophia looked horrified. "Imagine touching a poisoned apple!"

Emily giggled. "We'd all fall over and look as if we were dead, and have to wait to be kissed by a handsome—"

She was interrupted by a knock on the door, and Fairy Angora appeared. She's our school Fairy Godmother, and she keeps an eye on us all.

"Too much noise, my precious darlings," she said. "It's time to go to sleep!"

She waved her wand, and a drift of twinkly sparkles floated into the air...and I suddenly couldn't keep my eyes open a second longer.

Chapter Two

I had the weirdest dream! I was wearing a pair of absolutely gorgeous crystal slippers, and I was dancing all by myself in the middle of a huge ballroom...and then I felt someone shaking me.

"Alice! Wake up! Come on!" It was Charlotte. "The bell's gone – you've got to get up! It's the visit to the museum today – we've got to hurry!"

I forgot all about my dream, and ZOOMED out of bed.

Lady Albina fussed about giving out questionnaires and pencils and instructions all the time we were eating our breakfast. Honestly – it almost made me not want to go! Luckily Crown Prince Dandino came bouncing into the breakfast hall just as we finished. He organises our school outings, and he's good fun.

"Everyone ready for a fabulous day out?" he asked. "We'll be going to King Rudolfo's library first, to see some of his books. Then we'll visit the museum, and you can have a good look at the exhibits, and at the end of the morning we'll meet up back in the library. You can finish filling in your questionnaires while you're there. Lunch will be in the state dining room, and afterwards you can wander round the gardens while King Rudolfo and I look at your work. We'll announce the tiara points awarded and the winners of the competition at a little ceremony before we all go home!"

I was really glad when we finally rolled up the enormous drive to King Rudolfo's palace. All of us Silver Rose Roomers were in the same coach, and so were Princess Jemima, Princess Lisa, Princess

Freya and Princess Chloe. Unfortunately the twins were there as well – and Diamonde spent the whole journey telling us how she and Gruella had been to the museum before.

"Of course," Diamonde boasted, "we had tea with King Rudy, didn't we, Gruella?"

Gruella nodded enthusiastically. "King Rudy gave us FIFTEEN different kinds of cake."

"I thought he was called King Rudolfo," Emily said.

"He is, but his special friends call him King Rudy, and Mummy's one of his MOST special friends." Diamonde looked SO pleased with herself as she sat back, almost as if she was expecting a round of applause.

"That's nice," Daisy said, but she didn't sound very impressed. Diamonde leant forward, and went on boasting.

"AND he let us hold the pea that was under the mattresses, and look in the magic mirror, and do whatever we wanted. Didn't he, Gruella?"

Gruella nodded again, but it was odd. She was suddenly

looking a bit uncomfortable.

Diamonde coughed loudly. "AHEM! And do you know what else? King Rudy even let me try on the crystal slipper!"

"Goodness!" said Princess Chloe, and her eyes were very big and round. "Did he really?"

Diamonde smiled a self-satisfied smile. "It fitted me PERFECTLY."

I hadn't been paying her much attention, because I was wondering what was wrong with Gruella, but that made me sit up.

"You can't have worn the slipper," I said, surprised. "I SO want to try it, but my big sis told me nobody's EVER allowed to!"

Diamonde went bright red, and glared at me. "Well, I did! Didn't I, Gruella?" And I was sure I saw her pinch her twin.

"Oh – yes," Gruella said, and nodded hard.

"You'll see!" Diamonde hissed at me. "Just because you've got a big sister doesn't mean you know everything!"

I didn't answer. I was almost certain Diamonde had been telling fibs, and when I looked at my friends' faces I knew they thought so too.

Chapter Three

As soon as the coach stopped, Diamonde grabbed Gruella, and the two of them pushed their way out before the rest of us had even picked up our bags.

An incredibly tall, thin king wearing horn-rimmed spectacles was leaning against the wall, and Diamonde positively elbowed

Prince Dandino out of the way as she dashed towards him.

"King Rudy!" she squealed, and sank into a curtsey. "Mummy says she's just LONGING to see you again!"

A nasty little bit of me was hoping King Rudolfo would say,

"WHO? WHAT? Who are you?" but he didn't. He smiled a rather absent-minded smile, and said, "Many thanks, my dear – many thanks indeed." He took off his spectacles, cleaned them, then put them back on and peered at the rest of us.

"Welcome to you all," he said. "We'll start in the library, shall we?"

Number one on our questionnaire was, *"How many books are there in King Rudolfo's library?"*, and I was very glad we didn't have to count them, because there were thousands! He told us there were about fifty thousand, but he couldn't be certain.

"Excuse me, Your Majesty," I said, "but might I ask how many you've read?"

Diamonde gave a little shriek. "Oh! Alice! You can't mean your super special big sister didn't tell you? King Rudy's got MUCH more important things to do than read books – haven't you, King Rudy?"

King Rudolfo looked at Diamonde in a puzzled sort of way.

"Actually, my dear," he said, "I think reading is a totally delightful occupation. There isn't much you can't learn from a book. Now, shall I let you all have a wander round? My housekeeper will bring you something to drink very shortly." And he patted Diamonde on the head as he wandered away.

Diamonde looked cross for a moment, then waved her arm at the books as if they belonged to her.

"Shall I show you round?" she said. "After all, Gruella and I have been here before."

"No thank you," I said. "We'll look for ourselves." And I'm sorry if that sounded rude, but I was getting SO fed up with Diamonde being such a show-off.

"Oooooh," Diamonde sneered. "Guess who thinks her big sister has told her everything there is to know!"

I didn't answer. I took Charlotte's arm, and we went to look at a row of pictures of King Rudolfo's family. Daisy, Emily, Katie and Sophia came with us, and we studied the huge paintings carefully.

"Look!" Daisy said. "All King Rudolfo's relations are holding books!"

Katie chuckled. "So that's question number two answered. *How do King Rudolfo's family entertain themselves when they are at leisure?*"

"I do wish we could go to the museum," I said. "I'm dying to see the crystal slipper!"

And, just as if she'd heard me, at that moment the housekeeper came in with a tray of juice and biscuits.

"I've just opened the museum,' she announced as she put the tray down. "King Rudolfo says he'll be back in twenty minutes or so to show you round."

"Must we wait for him?"
I asked.

The housekeeper smiled at me.

"You can wait for him in the museum if you've finished here. It's just down the corridor and through the swing doors."

We looked at each other.

"Do you want a drink?" I asked. "Or shall we go now?"

"Let's go now!" Emily said, and Sophia, Daisy, Katie and Charlotte nodded.

Chapter Four

The museum wasn't very big, but it was absolutely crammed with glass cases, and the walls had shelves reaching right up to the ceiling. It was quite scary; the shelves were piled so high with papers and boxes and bits and pieces I couldn't help thinking we'd be totally buried if they fell down. It felt more like a workroom or a study than a museum, and we found ourselves whispering as we tiptoed round.

"Wow!" Charlotte was staring into a little silver casket. "Here's a pea! It says it's the actual pea the princess felt under all the mattresses!"

Sophia came to look. "It looks very shrivelled," she said doubtfully.

Katie pointed to a corner. "That looks like the spinning wheel!"

We went to look, and she was quite right. Beside it was a

40

tottering heap of pure gold plates, all with the most complicated royal crests.

"It says these came from Cinderella's wedding," Daisy whispered as she read the label.

"There's half an apple on that shelf," Katie whispered back. "Do you—"

She stopped, because Diamonde and Gruella were standing in the doorway...and there was something very sneaky about the way they were looking round.

We didn't mean to spy on them. We really really didn't – although I suppose if we'd been truly Perfect Princesses we'd have stepped forward as soon as we saw them and said hello. As it was, we stayed in our dark corner and watched to see what they were up to.

"King Rudy won't be here for at LEAST ten minutes," Diamonde said. "We've got LOADS of time." And she put up her hand and switched on the light.

It made SUCH a difference! There was a magnificent chandelier in the middle of the room, and it glittered and shone, and sent sparkles of light flashing over the glass cases. In particular it lit up a tall case that was immediately beneath, and I don't know why Diamonde and Gruella didn't hear us as we ooohed and aaaahed. The crystal slipper was SO gorgeous – I don't know how we could possibly have missed it when we first came in.

I was just moving out of our dark corner when Katie pulled me back.

"Look at Diamonde!" she hissed in my ear. I looked, and my mouth dropped WIDE open.

Diamonde was trying to lift up the glass cover over the crystal slipper!

"Here!" she snapped at Gruella. "Can't you see I need help?"

Gruella didn't look at all happy. "I don't think—" she began, but Diamonde took no notice.

"I told Chloe I'd worn the crystal slipper," she said, "and I'm going to wear it – so THERE!"

She gave the glass cover one last heave, lifted it off – and

DROPPED IT!

Splinters of glass flew everywhere, and the CRASH! was tremendous. Daisy screamed, and Emily shrieked, and Charlotte, Sophia, Katie and I gasped as we hurried out from behind the cases. At once Diamonde snatched up the slipper, and pushed it into my hands. When Prince Dandino and King Rudolfo came hurrying in a second later, followed by all the Silver Towers princesses, there I was – standing in the middle of a heap of shattered glass, and clutching the crystal slipper.

As everyone stared and stared and STARED at me Diamonde said, "She told us she'd always wanted to try on the slipper. We all heard her, didn't we Chloe?"

What could poor Chloe say? She went bright red, and nodded. Prince Dandino folded his arms, and frowned at me.

"I can't say how disappointed I am, Princess Alice. I've always thought of you as one of our star pupils, but this is a terrible TERRIBLE thing to have done!"

I didn't know what to do. I couldn't say it was Diamonde who had broken the glass case, because that would have been telling tales – and I knew my friends would feel exactly the same. I stared down at the crystal slipper, and I was so muddled and angry and embarrassed I began to blush.

"See?" Diamonde sounded triumphant. "She's going all red!"

"Princess Alice – I think you'd better go straight to the library," Prince Dandino said sternly. "And when we get back to Silver Towers we'll see what Queen Samantha Joy has to say."

"Yes, Your Highness," I said, and I was about to curtsey when I remembered I was still holding the crystal slipper. I held it out to King Rudolfo.

"Please excuse me, Your Majesty," I said. "And I am very VERY sorry that this has happened."

King Rudolfo took the slipper, and then he did SUCH an odd

thing. He gave me a little bow, and said, "Before you retire to the library, Princess Alice, would you like to try on the crystal slipper?"

I couldn't believe my ears. I was SO unprincessy! I really and truly gawped at him. Prince Dandino made a tut-tutting noise.

"I don't think Princess Alice deserves such an honour, Your Majesty," he said.

King Rudolfo gave a funny little smile, and said, "Please allow this, Prince Dandino. I have my reasons."

So I took off my shoe, and King Rudolfo slid the slipper onto my foot!

It was WEIRD. It fitted quite well, but it was a little bit tight round my heel – and it felt so cold and hard.

I couldn't imagine how anybody could have danced in a pair of crystal slippers. It only goes to show how very special the real owner must have been.

"Thank you," King Rudolfo said as he gently took the slipper off again. "And now, would anyone else like to try?"

Of   course   just   about

EVERYONE put their hands up. King Rudolfo beckoned to Diamonde.

"Why don't you try, Princess... oh, I'm so sorry." He shook his head. "I've forgotten your name."

Diamonde pouted, then smiled a forgiving smile. "I'm Queen Euphemia's daughter," she reminded him. "I'm Princess Diamonde. And I'd LOVE to try on the crystal slipper!"

Chapter Five

And that was when I had a BRILLIANT idea. I wasn't going to tell on Diamonde – but I WAS going to make sure she didn't get away with everything.

I swept King Rudolfo my very best curtsey, and I said, "Thank you for your kindness, King Rudolfo. It was most generous of you, and I have no right to ask anything of you – but as Princess Diamonde has already tried the slipper, might another princess have the honour, perhaps?"

King Rudolfo raised his eyebrows. "Princess Diamonde has already tried the slipper?"

If looks could kill, I'd have been flat on the floor. Diamonde GLARED at me as she said, "But I haven't, Your Majesty. Princess Alice must be mistaken."

"No she isn't!" It was little Princess Chloe. "You told us you did, Diamonde! When we were in the coach, remember? You said King Rudy had let you try on the slipper, and it fitted you perfectly!"

There was a long pause. It was SO obvious that Diamonde had been telling fibs. She went absolutely PURPLE, and shuffled her feet, and muttered about only pretending, and she hadn't really meant it.

King Rudolfo stroked his chin thoughtfully as he listened. Then he held the slipper out.

"Please put it on," he commanded.

Diamonde gulped. She took

the slipper, put it on – and immediately began to hop and skip all over the broken glass.

"HELP!" she squealed. "HELP! I can't STOP!" But it was no good. Round and round the glass cases she danced, spinning in circles.

"Princess Diamonde! STOP THIS MINUTE!" Prince Dandino roared, but it was no good. Poor Diamonde couldn't stop. King Rudolfo was frowning, but most of the Silver Towers princesses were laughing and laughing and LAUGHING. She did look funny – but it was horrible as well because she looked SO unhappy.

I ran to her, and took her hand.

"I'll help you," I said. "Hang on to me – try and kick the slipper off!"

But Diamonde couldn't. The next thing I knew I was hopping and skipping as well, and when

Charlotte grabbed me she began dancing too.

King Rudolfo held up his hand.

"I think," he said, "Princess Diamonde has something to say."

And Diamonde, puffing hard and bright red with her hair all over her face, panted, "It was ME! I broke the glass case! I'm very very sorry..."

She stopped at once, and

flopped against me. Charlotte and I almost had to hold her up.

Prince Dandino strode across the room looking REALLY angry, but I moved in front of Diamonde. I couldn't help it.

I knew she was a show-off and told boastful fibs, but I also knew how AWFUL it must have been having everyone laughing, and not being able to stop.

"Please," I said, "please don't be too cross with her. She didn't mean to break the glass, really she didn't."

King Rudolfo nodded.

"Princess Alice is quite right," he said. "Princess Diamonde has had punishment enough." He took my hand and kissed it.

"It's a delight to meet such a Perfect Princess."

"Me?" I said in surprise.

"A true princess never laughs at the misfortunes of others... however well deserved those misfortunes may be." For a second I thought I saw a tiny twinkle in his eye – but I might have been wrong. Then he went on.

"I suggest that Princess Alice's generosity is rewarded. Shall we forget the questionnaire, Prince Dandino, and ask Princess Alice and her friends to lead my Royal Parade tomorrow, and to ride in the Golden Pumpkin Coach?"

Chapter Six

So that was how Charlotte, Katie, Daisy, Sophia, Emily and I spent the next day...and it was GLORIOUS! We spent the whole morning getting ready (we were wearing our very best dresses, and then at exactly twelve o'clock the Golden Pumpkin Coach came rolling up to Silver Towers, pulled

by six gorgeous golden ponies.
We settled ourselves inside, and
then off we went...all the way

round the town, with the rest of
the Royal Parade marching and
dancing and singing behind us.

There were THOUSANDS of people watching, and we bowed and smiled until our faces were sore. And at the end of the day we went back to King Rudolfo's palace, and – guess what!

Yes – we had the most amazing tea, and there were THIRTY different kinds of cake. Charlotte and I counted them.

And just before we were finally driven back to Silver Towers the housekeeper gave us the left over cakes to share with all our other friends...

When it was bedtime, I found Diamonde waiting for me by Silver Rose Room door. She looked really awkward and embarrassed.

"Sorry," she mumbled – and then she was off down the stairs as fast as she could go.

And as I snuggled down in my bed, I thought how wonderful life was at Silver Towers...and I'm SO glad you're here with us.

What happens next?
Find out in

Princess Sophia

and the Prince's Party

Hello! I'm Princess Sophia,
and I'm a Tiara Club princess
here at Silver Towers – just like you!
And I'm SO glad you're here with us.
I expect you know my friends who share
Silver Rose Room with me. There's Alice,
and Daisy, and Katie and Charlotte and
Emily – and I just KNOW that if we
get enough Tiara Points to win our
Silver Sashes, and go on to Ruby Mansions
we'll still be the very best friends ever.
We're not too friendly with Princess
Diamonde and her twin sister Gruella,
though. They just LOVE showing off,
and being mean...

Check out

The Tiara Club

website at:

www.tiaraclub.co.uk

You'll find Perfect Princess games and fun things to do, as well as news on the Tiara Club and all your favourite princesses!

Win a Tiara Club
Perfect Princess Prize!

Look for the secret word in mirror writing hidden in a tiara in each of the Tiara Club books. Each book has one word. Put together the six words from books **7** to **12** to make a special Perfect Princess sentence, then send it to us together with 20 words or more on why you like the Tiara Club books. Each month, we will put the correct entries in a draw and one lucky reader will receive a magical Perfect Princess prize!

Send your Perfect Princess sentence, your name
and your address on a postcard to:
THE TIARA CLUB COMPETITION,
Orchard Books, 338 Euston Road,
London, NW1 3BH

Australian readers should write to:
Hachette Children's Books,
Level 17/207 Kent Street, Sydney, NSW 2000.

Only one entry per child.
Final draw: 31 August 2007

The Tiara Club

By Vivian French
Illustrated by Sarah Gibb

PRINCESS CHARLOTTE
AND THE BIRTHDAY BALL ISBN 1 84362 863 5
PRINCESS KATIE
AND THE SILVER PONY ISBN 1 84362 860 0
PRINCESS DAISY
AND THE DAZZLING DRAGON ISBN 1 84362 864 3
PRINCESS ALICE
AND THE MAGICAL MIRROR ISBN 1 84362 861 9
PRINCESS SOPHIA
AND THE SPARKLING SURPRISE ISBN 1 84362 862 7
PRINCESS EMILY
AND THE BEAUTIFUL FAIRY ISBN 1 84362 859 7

The Tiara Club at Silver Towers

PRINCESS CHARLOTTE
AND THE ENCHANTED ROSE ISBN 1 84616 195 9
PRINCESS KATIE
AND THE DANCING BROOM ISBN 1 84616 196 7
PRINCESS DAISY
AND THE MAGICAL MERRY-GO-ROUND ISBN 1 84616 197 5
PRINCESS ALICE
AND THE CRYSTAL SLIPPER ISBN 1 84616 198 3
PRINCESS SOPHIA
AND THE PRINCE'S PARTY ISBN 1 84616 199 1
PRINCESS EMILY
AND THE WISHING STAR ISBN 1 84616 200 9

All priced at £3.99.

The Tiara Club books are available from all good bookshops, or can be ordered direct
from the publisher: Orchard Books, PO BOX 29, Douglas IM99 1BQ.

Credit card orders please telephone 01624 836000 or fax 01624 837033 or visit our
Internet site: www.wattspub.co.uk or e-mail: bookshop@enterprise.net for details.

To order please quote title, author, ISBN and your full name and address.

Cheques and postal orders should be made payable to 'Bookpost plc.'

Postage and packing is FREE within the UK
(overseas customers should add £2.00 per book).

Prices and availability are subject to change.